Revised Edition

FIREFLIES
IN THE
NIGHT

by Judy Hawes

illustrated by Ellen Alexander

HarperCollins*Publishers*

Fireflies in the Night
Text copyright © 1963, 1991 by Judy Hawes
Illustrations copyright © 1991 by Ellen Alexander
Manufactured in China. For information address
HarperCollins Children's Books, a division of HarperCollins Publishers,
10 East 53rd Street, New York, NY 10022.
Revised Edition

Library of Congress Cataloging-in-Publication Data
Hawes, Judy.
   Fireflies in the night / by Judy Hawes ; illustrated by Ellen
Alexander. — Rev. ed.
      p.   cm. — (Let's-read-and-find-out science. Stage 1)
   Summary: Describes how and why fireflies make their light, how to
catch and handle them, and several uses for firefly light.
   ISBN 0-06-022484-3. — ISBN 0-06-022485-1 (lib. bdg.)
   ISBN 0-06-445101-1 (pbk.)
   1. Fireflies—Juvenile literature.   [1. Fireflies.]   I. Alexander, Ellen, ill.
II. Title.   III. Series.
QL596.L28H38   1991   90-1587
595.76′44—dc20   CIP
                                                                  AC

The illustrations were done in pastels on Rives smooth watercolor paper.
09 10 11 12 13 SCP 20 19 18 17 16 15 14 13 12 11

FIREFLIES
IN THE
NIGHT

I like fireflies. When I visit my grandfather in the summertime, we sit outdoors after supper and watch them.

Grandmother likes to watch fireflies too. She calls them
lightning bugs. They look like little dancing stars. They are
really beetles, Grandfather says.

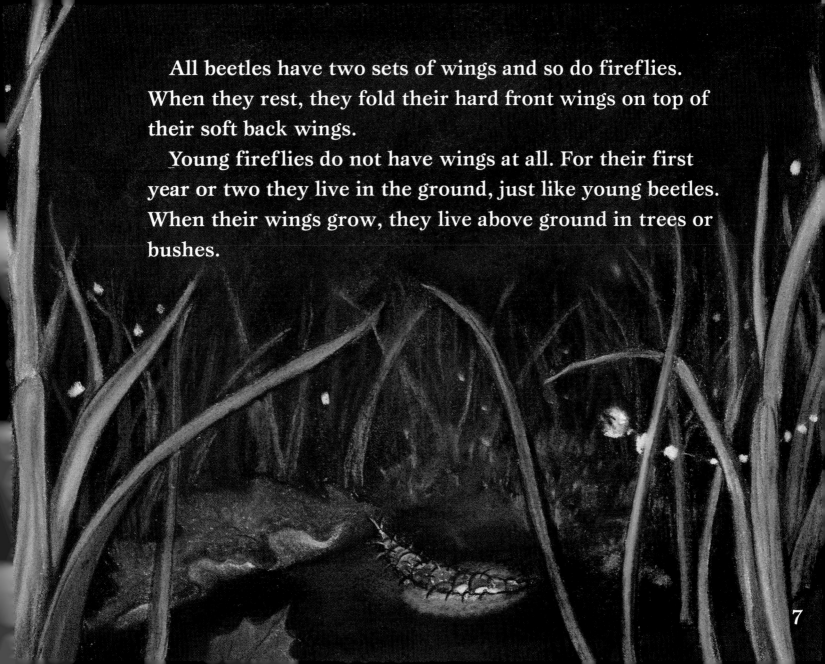

All beetles have two sets of wings and so do fireflies.
When they rest, they fold their hard front wings on top of
their soft back wings.

Young fireflies do not have wings at all. For their first
year or two they live in the ground, just like young beetles.
When their wings grow, they live above ground in trees or
bushes.

Grandfather gave me a glass jar to use on firefly hunts. We punched holes in the lid.

Fireflies are easy to catch. Soon my jar is lighted up like a lantern.

After every firefly hunt, Grandfather has something
new to tell me. One time he showed me how to make my
firefly lantern brighter. (He promised it would not hurt my
fireflies.) Just hold the jar upright in a bowl of warm water.

He knew it would work because fireflies always shine brighter in warm weather. If you dip the jar in cold water, the firefly lights will fade.

People in hot countries make good use of firefly light. In the Caribbean, and in some parts of South America, people sometimes wear net bags full of fireflies tied to their wrists or ankles. These homemade flashlights help them find their way along the dark jungle paths.

Grandfather let me try this in the cornfield because we have no jungle.

In Japan, the gardens are lighted at night by firefly lanterns. That must be nice!

Grandfather also told me about a doctor in Cuba who, many years ago, once used a firefly lamp in his operating room. His other lights had gone out!

Fireflies make *cold* light. Candles make hot light. If I put one tiny birthday candle in a jar, the jar gets too hot to hold. My firefly lantern never gets warm.

I asked my grandfather, "How can fireflies make cold light?" He told me that fireflies have special chemicals inside them. When fireflies take in air, the air mixes with these chemicals. Flash!—the mixture makes light *without heat*.

AIR   AIR

    Small holes on the side of the firefly let air in. The special chemicals mix with air in the underpart of the firefly. These chemicals plus air equal cold light.

Fireflies have special ways to flash their lights which they repeat over and over. Each kind signals in a different pattern of flashes and pauses. As he flies around, a male firefly may make a signal like this: 3 or 4 or 5 quick flashes. Wait for six seconds. Repeat.

A female firefly stays in the grass and gives her own kind of answering signal, probably like this: 1, 2, or 3 quick flashes. Wait for two seconds. Repeat. That's how fireflies find their mates.

Grandfather says if I sit quietly in the grass and flash a small flashlight on and off every two seconds, the fireflies may be fooled and come to *me*! I am going to try that tomorrow night.

Tonight I am taking my firefly lantern to my secret hideaway. Under the bedcovers my lantern makes a cozy light. Just for me!

My grandmother will come soon to say goodnight.

"Lights out," Grandmother will say. She will take my lantern outside and let my fireflies go.

I'll catch some more tomorrow night.